A GIFT FOR:

....

FROM:

....

How to Use Your Interactive Storybook & Story Buddy™:

1. Activate your Story Buddy™ by pressing the "On / Off" button on the ear.
2. Read the story aloud in a quiet place. Speak in a clear voice when you see the highlighted phrases.
3. Listen to your Story Buddy™ respond with several different phrases throughout the book.

Clarity and speed of reading affect the way Scooby-Doo™ responds.
He may not always respond to young children.

Watch for even more interactive Storybooks & Story Buddy™ characters.
For more information, visit us on the Web at Hallmark.com/StoryBuddy.

TM & © Hanna-Barbera.
(s12)

Copyright © 2012 Hallmark Licensing, LLC

Published in 2012 by Hallmark Gift Books,
a division of Hallmark Cards, Inc.
Kansas City, MO 64141
Visit us on the Web at Hallmark.com.

Editor: Emily Osborn
Designer: Mark Voss
Art Director: Kevin Swanson
Production Artist: Dan Horton

ISBN: 978-1-59530-470-4
KOB9048

Printed and bound in China
SEP12

I Reply ™
TECHNOLOGY

Hallmark's **I Reply Technology** brings your Story Buddy™ to life! When you read the key phrases out loud, your Story Buddy™ gives a variety of responses, so each time you read feels as magical as the first.

BOOK 2

SCOOBY-DOO!™

AND THE MYSTERIOUS MAP

Hallmark
gift books

BY ANDRE DU BROC • ILLUSTRATED BY RICHARD LAPIERRE

It was everyone's favorite time of year—the annual Coolsville County Fair! And the Mystery Inc. gang was having a great time exploring.

Fred loved the games. Daphne loved the beautiful plants and flowers.

Velma liked the music most of all. Shaggy and Scooby, of course, loved
the food. They loved fair food almost as much as they loved a good mystery.

Shaggy and Scooby shared a super-duper ice-cream sundae. They made quite a mess, too. Shaggy grabbed a napkin to clean his face.

But it wasn't a napkin at all. It looked like a piece of a map. It looked like a mystery.

"Let's get the gang together, Scooby!" Shaggy said.

The gang looked at the piece of paper. "It's an old treasure map," said Velma. "Treasure!" Shaggy and Scooby shouted excitedly.

"Looks like we need to find a bear," said Fred, pointing to the map.
"And I know just the place. Follow me! We've got a mystery to solve!"

Fred led the gang to the basketball toss.
"Teddy bears are the prizes," said Fred.
"Jinkies! But there's so many!" said Velma.

"What about this one?" asked Daphne.
She held up a big blue one. Another bit of
paper was underneath it. This mysterious map
was certainly making the day exciting.

The gang gathered around the second piece. It fit just right with the first.

"Looks like a purple sun," said Velma.

"Or . . . it could be a flower!" said Daphne.
The gang followed her through the crowd to a tent
filled with beautiful plants. The gang was amazed.

"Zoinks! It'll be hard to find our flower in here," said Shaggy. Then Scooby's face lit up.

He spotted the purple flower!

He dashed over to it as fast as he could.

Velma picked up the flowerpot. A bit of paper was
stuck underneath. It was another piece of the
mysterious map. And it fit with the other two pieces!
This one showed a big red dragon.

"ZOINKS!"

said Shaggy. "Does this mean we need to find a dragon?"
Scooby and Shaggy were scared.

"I think I know where we can find that big red dragon," said Velma.
"And there's no reason to be scared. Follow me!"

The gang raced behind Velma toward the big stage where a band was playing. They stopped right in front of the stage. The gang was amazed.

There was a red dragon on the band's bass drum.

"How are we going to get up on the stage?" asked Daphne.

"Leave that to Scooby," said Shaggy, grinning.

The band finished playing and took a short break. While they were gone, Scooby sneaked up onto the stage and behind the drum set. He knew he was supposed to look for the map, but instead, Scooby picked up the drumsticks and started pounding on the drums. Suddenly the audience cheered loudly.

Just then the lights came up. Since the crowd was
already clapping, Scooby played a little drum solo.

Then Scooby grabbed the piece of paper and sneaked back offstage.

This type of fun made Scooby laugh out loud.

Scooby showed the gang the piece of the map he had found.
This one was a little different from the others.

It had a big X on it. They hoped that's where they would find the treasure!
The thought of finding it was certainly making the day exciting!

"It looks like X marks the spot," said Velma.

"Yeah," said Daphne, "but where are we going to find a big X?"

The gang thought and thought but couldn't figure this one out.

They decided to take a break and ride the Ferris wheel.

And that's when they saw their X.
The treasure was right in the middle of town!
After the gang finished their ride, they ran
down to where the two streets crossed.

But when they got there, it wasn't exactly a treasure they found . . .
but it was exciting! Especially for Scooby!

"Hey, kids!" said the man behind the counter. "Glad to see you
found our scavenger hunt map!"

"Scavenger hunt?" Fred asked.

"That's right!" the other man replied. "We hid flyers at all of our other places at the fair! To lead people here, to our new shop!"

"Hmm," said Velma. "That must make you the Jones brothers."

"That's us! And since you're the first to find all the pieces of the map, you get a free box of Scooby Snacks!"

"Scooby-Dooby-Doo!" cheered Scooby.

"Like, wow, Scooby!" Shaggy said. "Two of your favorite things in just one day!"

It was true. Scooby loved chowing down on Scooby Snacks,
but he really loved a good mystery!

IF YOU HAVE ENJOYED READING WITH SCOOBY-DOO™, WE WOULD LOVE TO HEAR FROM YOU!

Please send your comments to:
Hallmark Book Feedback
P.O. Box 419034
Mail Drop 215
Kansas City, MO 64141

Or e-mail us at:
booknotes@hallmark.com